BIG SAM

A ROSH HASHANAH TALL TALE

by Eric A. Kimmel

illustrated by Jim Starr

Springfield NJ · Jerusalem

For Gayle and Mike Klaybor –EK

For my Dad, who is my Big Sam –JS

Apples & Honey Press ∣ An imprint of Behrman House and Gefen Publishing House
Behrman House, 11 Edison Place, Springfield, New Jersey 07081 ∣ Gefen Publishing House Ltd., 6 Hatzvi Street, Jerusalem 94386, Israel
www.applesandhoneypress.com

Text copyright © 2017 by Eric A. Kimmel ∣ Illustrations copyright © 2017 by Jim Starr

ISBN 978-1-68115-525-8

Library of Congress Cataloging-in-Publication Data

Names: Kimmel, Eric A., author. ∣ Starr, Jim, 1960- illustrator.
Title: Big Sam : a Rosh Hashanah tall tale / by Eric A. Kimmel ; illustrated
   by Jim Starr.
Description: Springfield, NJ : Apples & Honey Press, [2017] ∣ Summary:
   Digging the Grand Canyon to use as a mixing bowl, a giant bakes an
   enormous challah for Rosh Hashanah and cleans up the environment
   afterwards.
Identifiers: LCCN 2016045326 ∣ ISBN 9781681155258 (alk. paper)
Subjects: ∣ CYAC: Rosh ha-Shanah--Fiction. ∣ Challah (Bread)--Fiction. ∣
   Bread--Fiction. ∣ Giants--Fiction. ∣ Tall tales.
Classification: LCC PZ7.K5648 Bi 2017 ∣ DDC [E]--dc23
LC record available at https://lccn.loc.gov/2016045326

Design by Virtual Paintbrush. ∣ Art Direction by Ann D. Koffsky. ∣ Edited by Dena Neusner
Printed in China.

1 3 5 7 9 8 6 4 2

Samson the Giant — Big Sam to his friends —
looked at the calendar. "It's almost time for
Rosh Hashanah, the New Year.
I'd better get started."

"I'll need to bake a special challah bread for Rosh Hashanah," said Big Sam. He dug a **big hole** in the ground to make a mixing bowl. It's still there today. We call it the Grand Canyon.

Big Sam filled the hole with a mountain of flour, tons of sugar,
barrels of yeast, a lake of oil, thousands of eggs, and a shovelful of salt.

"I'll need water, **lots** of it," said Big Sam. He dammed the Colorado River to make it flow through the canyon. It still flows through the Grand Canyon today.

Big Sam hiked over to the redwood forests in California.
He found a **giant** redwood blown over by a storm.

He whittled it into the shape of a spoon.

Big Sam started stirring. He mixed together all the flour, eggs, sugar, yeast, salt, oil, and water.

"Time to knead the dough," said Big Sam. He lifted the dough out of the Grand Canyon and carried it over to West Texas. He **stomped** down the hills to flatten the ground for kneading the dough. Parts of West Texas are still flat to this day.

Big Sam laid down the dough and started kneading it. He pushed and pulled. He lifted it up and **slammed** it down.

The dough began to feel light and smooth. Big Sam carried it up the Yellowstone River to a place where the ground steamed and smoked. Big Sam set the dough down near the geysers and let it rise.

The dough rose in the warm steam until it was **twice as big** as before. Big Sam punched it down until the earth shook. He rolled the dough into a long rope.

He wound the rope around and around and around to make a coil. Big Sam let the dough rise again until it was **nearly as big** as he was.

"Almost done," said Big Sam. "Now I'll brush the challah with egg yolks to make it brown and shiny. And I'll sprinkle it with poppy seeds."

Big Sam had plenty of eggs left. But his poppy seed jar was empty.

Big Sam ran to the rail yard in Denver. "I need poppy seeds. I'll take all you have," he told the train workers.

The train workers shook their heads. "Can't help you, Big Sam. We're out of poppy seeds. We're out of everything. Haven't you heard? The Mississippi River's flooded. The rail bridge is out. Nothing's getting through."

"When will it be fixed?" Big Sam asked.

The train workers shrugged. "Who knows? Three months? It's a disaster."

Big Sam moaned. "I can't wait three months. It will be Hanukkah by then. I'd better see what I can do."

Big Sam hiked over to the Mississippi River. He saw the high water carrying trees and houses. The railroad bridge had fallen down. The tracks were underwater. Trains lined up along the tracks, unable to cross.

"Can you help us, Big Sam?" the engineers asked.

Big Sam waded into the river. "Get ready, everybody," he said. "When I say go, GO!"
Big Sam crouched down. He lifted the train tracks and put them on his shoulders.
Then he hollered, **"Go!"**

The trains started up. One by one, they crossed the mighty Mississippi on
Big Sam's shoulders.

Everyone cheered for Big Sam. **"Hip, hip, hooray!"**

Big Sam headed back to Yellowstone with two boxcars of poppy seeds. He broke the eggs into Yellowstone Gorge and mixed them up with his redwood spoon.

He pulled a fir tree out of the ground to make a brush. He brushed the egg onto the challah and sprinkled poppy seeds over it. He had just enough!

"I'd better order three boxcars of poppy seeds next year," said Big Sam.

Big Sam carried the challah up to Mount Saint Helens. He stuck his hand into the crater. It felt nice and warm inside the volcano. **Perfect for baking!**

Big Sam pulled the top off Mount Saint Helens. He gently set the challah on the lava bed. Then he put the mountaintop back on.

"A challah that big will take a couple of days to bake," said Big Sam. "I'll gather apples and honey while I wait." He went to his orchard. The trees were full of juicy red apples. Streams of honey flowed from the beehives.

"We've been busy," the bees buzzed.

"Good job, bees," said Big Sam. "We're sure to have a happy and sweet year."

Big Sam came back a few days later to check his challah.
There it was—beautiful, golden, **enormous!**

"There's enough for everybody. Let's celebrate the New Year.
Come and eat!" Big Sam hollered.

Two bald eagles circled Big Sam's head. "Not so fast, Big Sam!" the eagles called. "You dropped a mountaintop on our forest. You knocked down our trees. You flattened our hills. You blocked our rivers. Didn't you think about the creatures who live here? What will we do now?"

Big Sam felt bad. He thought of the destruction he'd caused without thinking. **"I'm sorry,"** he told the eagles and all the other creatures who had lost their homes.

"I forgot that Rosh Hashanah is about mending the world. Whatever I did wrong, I'll make right. I'll do it now."

Big Sam rolled up his sleeves. He planted trees and flowers in the Grand Canyon wherever trees and flowers could go.

He filled the flat Texas prairie with wildflowers and grasses.

He cleared away the boulders that blocked the rivers. He dug and cleared and planted until the forest looked the way it had before.

"Thank you, Big Sam!" the eagles cried as they flew off to their nest.

"Thank you for letting me make our world better," Big Sam said.

"Now let's eat!"

People came from all over to join Big Sam. Paul Bunyan hiked down from the North Woods with his blue ox, Babe. Pecos Bill and Slue Foot Sue rode up from Texas. John Henry, the steel-driving man, brought his whole family from West Virginia. Annie Christmas and her crew poled their flatboat all the way up the Mississippi River.

They all came to share Big Sam's challah, to eat apples and honey, and to celebrate Rosh Hashanah together.

"*Shanah tovah!*" said Big Sam to his friends. "Here's to a happy and sweet year. For us, and for everyone all over the world."

QUESTIONS TO TALK ABOUT

Are there really giants in Jewish legends?

Yes! Big Sam follows a long tradition of Jewish stories about giants. In the Bible, we can read about the story of Samson, the strongest man who ever lived. There's also a legend about Og, a giant who survived the Flood by riding on the roof of Noah's Ark. And don't forget Goliath, the Philistine giant who battled with David.

Paul Bunyan, the giant logger; Pecos Bill, the giant cowboy; John Henry, the steel-driving man; and the rest of Big Sam's friends are larger-than-life figures from American folklore.

What makes a person a hero?

Being a hero isn't about strength or size. It's about caring for others, taking responsibility for our actions, and making sure the world is a fit place for all of us to live in.

There is a Jewish value called *tikkun olam*, which means "mending the world." Big Sam restores the forest and the streams he has damaged while making his challah, thereby fulfilling the concept of *tikkun olam*.

Why is Rosh Hashanah a good time to read and think about this story?

Just as Sam looked back at his actions, Rosh Hashanah is a time for us to look back at our actions from the past year, too.

- What things have you done that you are proud of?
- How can you do more things like them?
- What would you like to change?
- How can you get started?